Cinderella Christmas

by Elizabeth Chapin-Pinotti

Cinderella Christmas
Text and illustrations 2014 © Elizabeth Chapin-Pinotti
First Print Edition Plymouth, CA
SBN-13: 978-0692337035 ISBN-10:0692337032

Once upon a time, in the deepest, darkest, farthest reaches of the North Pole, a lovely little elf Princess lived a happy, Christmasy life with her father.

Princess Charity was a special elf for she was the only daughter of the Elf King Patience.

King Patience was a handsome and beloved elf, well handsome as far as elves go. He was stout and round and had the magical elfin ability to grow bigger or smaller – as the situation called for. Princess Charity loved helping her father deck the halls and the trees and the houses and everything else that needed decking for Christmas.

To Do
1 Trim Trees
2 Polish Rudolph's Nose
3 Supervise Toy Making
4 Trim Prancer's Hooves
5 Check GPS on the sleigh
6 Paint Candy Janes

The King was a joyful elf in charge of all that was Christmasy at the North Pole. This important and rather large task meant long hours and very few days off. Charity never knew her mother, but was told the queen of the elves had a fabulous, magical and super secret job, just like the princess' father, and in due time that secret would be revealed and something special would happen.

King Patience was encouraging to
all of the helper elves. "Turn them
brighter, my boy!"

"String them higher!"

"Make it bolder!"

"And...paint that fire engine redder, son!"
King Patience would say as he bustled through the village.

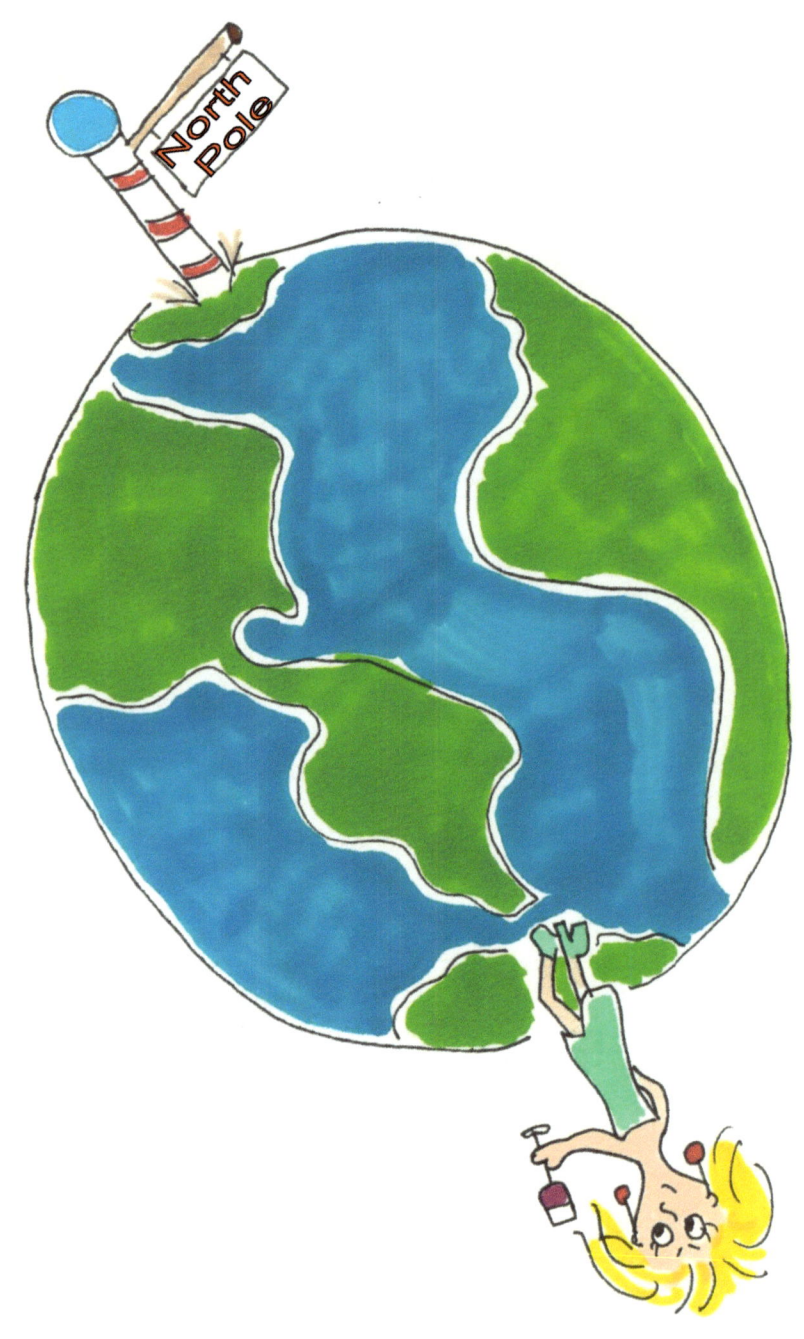

In order to best care for his precious and precocious little princess, King Patience decided he would marry again and set out to find a wife. He settled on a lady-in-waiting from the South Pole he'd met on the Polernet. Her name: Lady Shady from the South Pole Baby.

Lady Shady, a widow herself – was like nothing Princess Charity, or any of the NP elves, had ever seen. She was tall and thin and loved biscuits and gravy.

Princess Charity liked her very much, until Lady Shady married her father and then everything changed. Not only was Lady Shady as mean as Hades, she was the most horrible horror of horrors – Lady Shady from the South Pole Baby and her two daughters, Sadie and Brady, hated Christmas.

With King Patience away at the Christmas castle, readying for the season of giving, Lady Shady and her two daughters, Sadie and Brady tortured the poor elf princess.

The wild little ladies ran through the house – toppling the trees, smudging the stars and cracking candy canes.

"Clean up the
ornaments!"
"Polish the stars!"
"And glue those candy
canes back together!" they
yelled to Princess Charity.

"And stop that sickly singing!" yelled the Lady Shady – who was allergic to music.

The truth was, Princess Charity had a beautiful voice and she loved to sing Christmas Carols.

Day and night, night and day – while she cleaned and cooked and sewed and even while she polished Lady Shady's toes – Princess Charity would sing away happily – one Christmasy tune or another.

The closer it got to Christmas, the louder and happier she sang.

One day King Patience came home and announced that Santa was going to select someone from the North Pole to fulfill the most important position in all the land – the keeper of the naughty and nice list.

"Gather round family, Shady, Sadie, Brady and my one and only Princess Charity," the King said. "Santa has announced that he will hold a winter wonderland ball tonight in order to select the next keeper of the naughty and nice list."

Princess Charity's eyes grew wide, but Lady Shady pushed her aside.

"What does it all mean my king?" Lady Shady from the South Pole baby faked a syrupy smile.

"My dear, the keeper of the naughty and nice list is the highest honor in all of the North Pole. The king has also announced that the princess selected as the keeper will also wed his son."

"I *am* a princess by marriage now.
Aren't I mother?" Sadie said with her eye
on the prize.

Brady elbowed her sister.
"I am too, besides I'm older," she
said smiling sweetly at the king.

"You are the King elf," Lady Shady from the South Pole baby said, "second only to Santa. You must make my daughters officially princesses and then make sure one of them marries Santa's son."

At that point, the elf king decided to grow small. His wife liked it when he was small and he wanted to distract her – for King Patience had other plans.

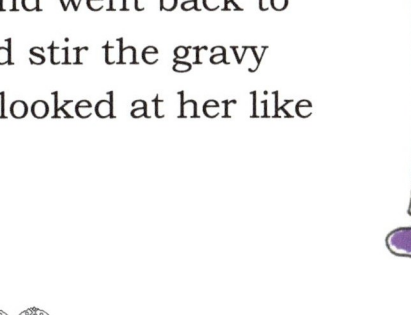

"Wonder if Steven knows his dad's trying to marry him off?" mumbled Charity. "Can't imagine he'd be too happy about it."

The princess shrugged her shoulders, grabbed some candy, jumped over Sadie and went back to the kitchen to flip the biscuits and stir the gravy while her stepmother and sisters looked at her like she was crazy.

She was stirring the pot,
singing a catchy holiday tune
and staring out of window
when a buzzering bee landed
on the 'sill.

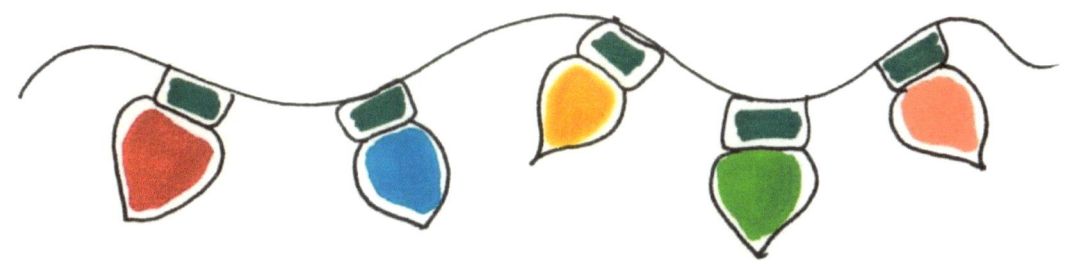

Charity was about to swat it with a towel when the bee began to speak.

"Woah!" the bee put up its little hands.

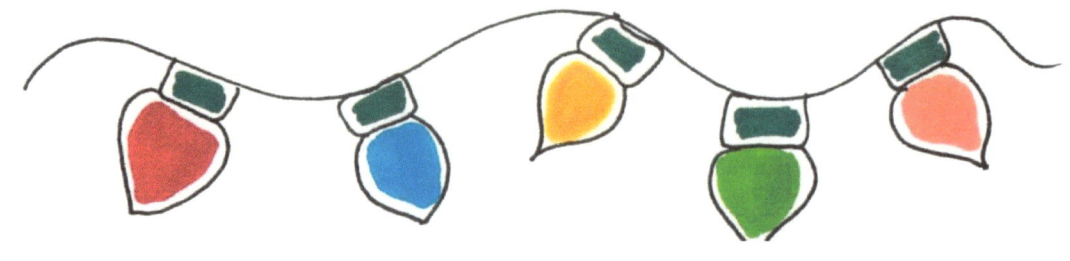

"Oh, sorry Mrs. Bee – I didn't know you were…"

"Were what? Alive? The flying didn't give it away?" she grumbled.

"You can speak!" exclaimed the Princess.

"Of course I can speak. This is the North Pole! We're all magical here…except when we're not."

"I suppose so," Charity said a bit confused by the comment. "Can I help you with something?"

"I'm here to help you," the bee landed on Charity's nose and looked into her eyes.

It was rather uncomfortable for the Princess, but being polite, she did not say a word, only crossed her eyes and tried to focus.

"Look, we've all heard the stories about Cinderella...where the beautiful princess' invitation to the ball is lost and at the last minute, a magical fairy godmother appears – bibs, bods and boos – and Cinderella is ready for the ball, goes to the ball, wins over the prince and lives happily ever after."

"Well yes." Then it struck her. "Are you my fairy godmother?"

The funny little bee fell backwards, laughing uproariously. "I'm here to tell you, there is no such thing!"

"Of course there is," Charity answered.

"Actually no...there isn't. It's all a sham...a ruse...to hold you back! Wise up! Nothing worth gettin' is easy to get. If you want that job and that prince to be yours...stop waiting on the Shady Lady and her crazy babies and get out there and make it happen."

"But the stories?" the princess stammered.

"Do you want the job or not?" the bee demanded.

"Of course. I suppose, yes," Charity replied.

"This is the real world, Princess. No one is going to make it happen but you...now go find a dress...polish up your pumpkin and get that job."

Charity turned and the bee buzzed backwards.

"Sorry!" the Princess said earnestly.

"No worries. Just do me a favor. No losing shoes or leaving trinkets...if you want the prince to remember you, be memorable," the bee stated. "Seriously, do you want to spend your life with someone who needs to fit a shoe on your foot because he can't remember what you look like?"

Now most of Charity's things had been taken by her stepsisters, but out in her father's Christmas Candy shed, under the smooth caramel and the succulently, sweet, sugary treats, in a top secret room, were trunks and trunks of her mother's ball gowns and jewels and crowns and power tools – not for balls but for cutting down Christmas trees – but that's another story all together.

She found a voluminous, violet gown of Vichi velvet and knew she'd struck gold, for everyone knew Vichi velvet was lucky.

"If I don't get a fairy godmother in all of this," Charity said to herself, "I'd better make a bit of luck! It's not so much for Santa's son Steven, but I'd really like to be in charge of the whole naughty and nice thing."

And off she went to get ready for the ball…without the help of mice or magic or pumpkins.

The Christmas Castle was near her house, so Charity hitched up a sleigh, called in a favor from Rudolph and flew on over to Santa's brilliant ball to have a blast...and maybe land her dream job.

The festivities were in full swing when the Princess entered the
room. She bowed before Santa and he kissed her head.

"Ho-ho-ho, Princess," Santa laughed like a bowl full of jelly, "I was
hoping you'd come."

The jolly old man, took her hand and whisked her around the dance floor before handing her off to his stupendously, sweet son Steven.

One look at the little elf all decked out in her beautiful ball gown and Steven's heart went thump, thump, thump.

Princess Charity'd always thought Steven was cool, but marriage?

She'd have to think about that one...if...of course...it even came to that.

Charity and Steven bopped and boogied the night away.
No one else could even get near the Prince of Christmas!

When the clock struck twelve Santa and Steven climbed up on stage. The gumdrop dancers stopped their jitterbug when Santa raised his arms.

"Citizens of the North Pole and members of the Court of the Christmas Castle," his cheeks grew rosy and his blue eyes twinkled. "The time has come to select a new keeper of the naughty and nice list. Mrs. Claus has done a marvelous job since we lost our last keeper, but her baking has suffered and poor old Santa is losing weight."

The crowd roared and everyone laughed. Santa was not losing weight.

Lady Shady had been watching Steven and Charity all night long and she was not happy. She pushed her stepdaughter behind her flowy skirts and made Brady and Sadie smile pretty.

Santa was not fooled.

The crowd cheered when the grand announcement
was made.

The princess joined them on stage.

"Ho, ho, ho!" Santa laughed, "Your mother would be proud. I have had my eye on you for a long time child, to make sure you had what it takes...like she did."

"Like she did...you mean?"

"Yes," said Santa. "Your mother was the keeper of the naughty and nice list for a very long time and now it is your turn."

Her father and Steven were as pleased as punch!

They decided on a long engagement...so Charity could concentrate on her new position.

Christmas was coming after all...and someone had to determine who was naughty and who was nice!

Princess Charity put her stepmother to work counseling the kids on the naughty list – including her stepsisters! Charity believed in reform and felt both sides deserved their time together!

And they all lived happily ever after…well most of the time anyway!

www.ingramcontent.com/pod-product-compliance
Lightning Source LLC
Chambersburg PA
CBHW041002170626
46815CB00002B/124